MICHAEL
MONSTERS

For Laura, Angela and Stuart

Copyright ©1996 by Gus Clarke.
This paperback edition first published in 2001 by Andersen Press Ltd.
The rights of Gus Clarke to be identified as the author and illustrator of this work
have been asserted by him in accordance with the Copyright, Designs and Patents Act, 1988.
First published in Great Britain in 1996 by Andersen Press Ltd., 20 Vauxhall Bridge Road, London SW1V 2SA.
Published in Australia by Random House Australia Pty., 20 Alfred Street, Milsons Point, Sydney, NSW 2061.
All rights reserved. Colour separated in Italy by Fotoriproduzioni Grafiche, Verona. Printed and bound in China.

10 9 8 7 6 5 4 3 2 1

British Library Cataloguing in Publication Data available.

ISBN 0 86264 723 1

This book has been printed on acid-free paper

MICHAEL'S MONSTERS

Gus Clarke

ANDERSEN PRESS · LONDON

"Quick!" said Michael. "Stand at the bottom of the stairs."

"No," said his dad. "You don't need me again."

"Please. I'm scared."

"No," said his mum. "There's nothing up there to be frightened of."

"Pleeeeeease."

"No," said his brother. "Why should I?"

"I'll wet myself," said Michael.

And there had been times when he did.

But most of the time he didn't. Because in the end, somebody *would* go and stand at the bottom of the stairs.

"What is it you're scared of up there?" said Mum.

"Monsters," said Michael.

"No such things," said Dad. "Come upstairs and show me some of these monsters."

"There's one," said Michael. "It's the Airing-cupboard Monster."

"Nonsense," said Dad. "You're imagining things."

"Well, there *is* one in *there*," said Michael. "It's the Under-the-bed Monster."

"Don't be silly," said Dad. "There's always a simple explanation. Any more?"

"Yes," said Michael. "The Wardrobe Monster."

"Hello, Wardrobe Monster. Pleased to meet you," said Dad.
"Is that all of them?"

"Nearly," said Michael. "There's the Next-door-to-the-bathroom Monster. Be careful."

"Don't worry," said Dad. "I've met this one before. He doesn't scare me and he shouldn't scare you."

"There," said Dad. "Now run along and we'll have no more of this nonsense. I'll be down in a minute."

"I'm cured!" said Michael. "There *are* no monsters."

"Well done, Michael," said Mum. "And well done, Dad."

"There never *were* any," said Michael.

"Aargh!...Quick! Stand at the bottom of the stairs...

. . ." said Dad.